www.mascotbooks.com

JURNI

©2020 Nikos Cox. All Rights Reserved. No part of this publication may be reproduced, stored in a retrieval system or transmitted in any form by any means electronic, mechanical, or photocopying, recording or otherwise without the permission of the author.

For more information, please contact:
Mascot Books
620 Herndon Parkway, Suite 320
Herndon, VA 20170
info@mascotbooks.com

Library of Congress Control Number: 2019917006

CPSIA Code: PRT0120A
ISBN-13: 978-1-64543-241-8

Printed in the United States

There were a million billion stars.

How would I ever find her?

At school, Mr. Maze says NASA is hosting a contest.

All my best ideas go in my journal.

I'll be an astronaut and explore all the stars.

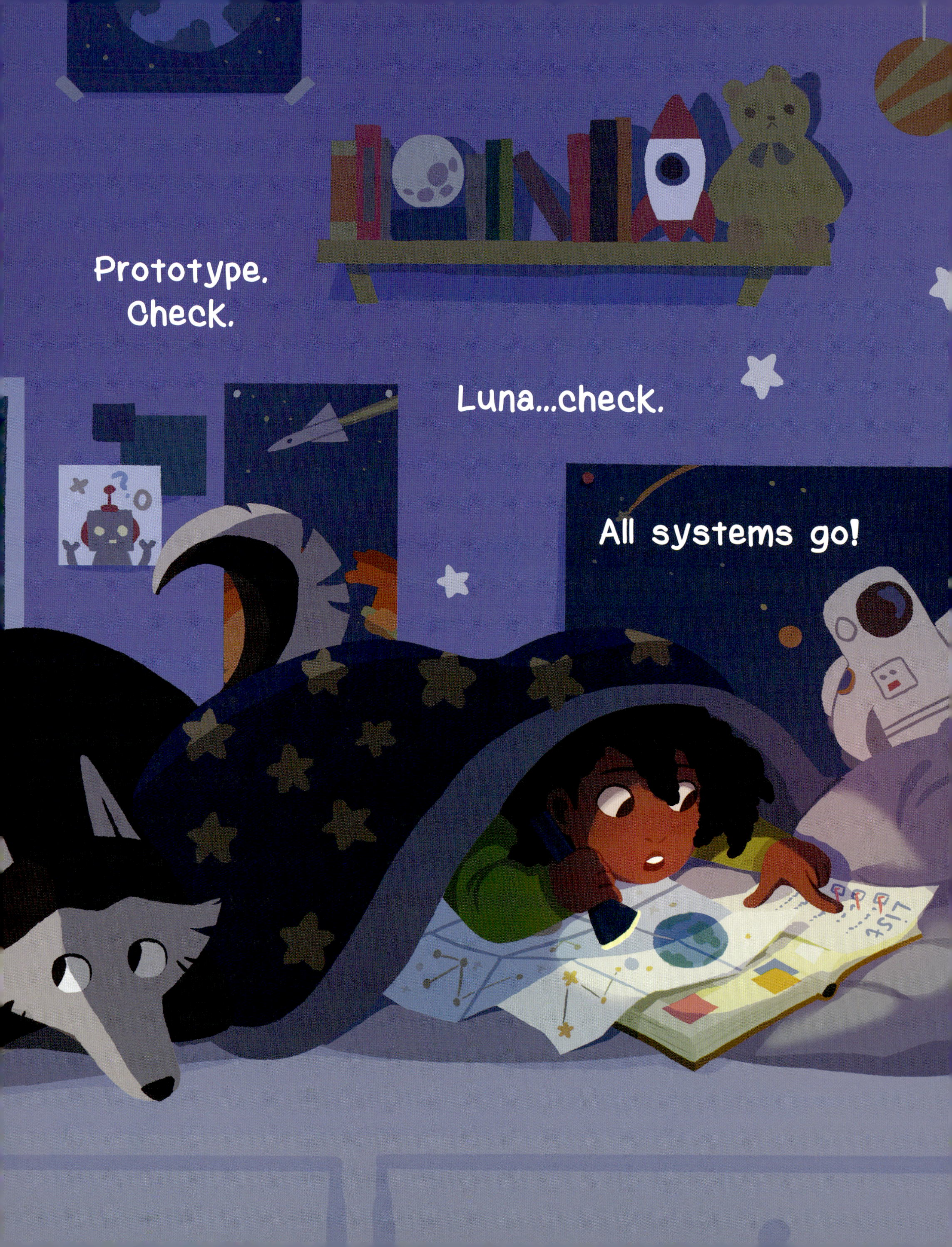

Prototype.
Check.

Luna...check.

All systems go!

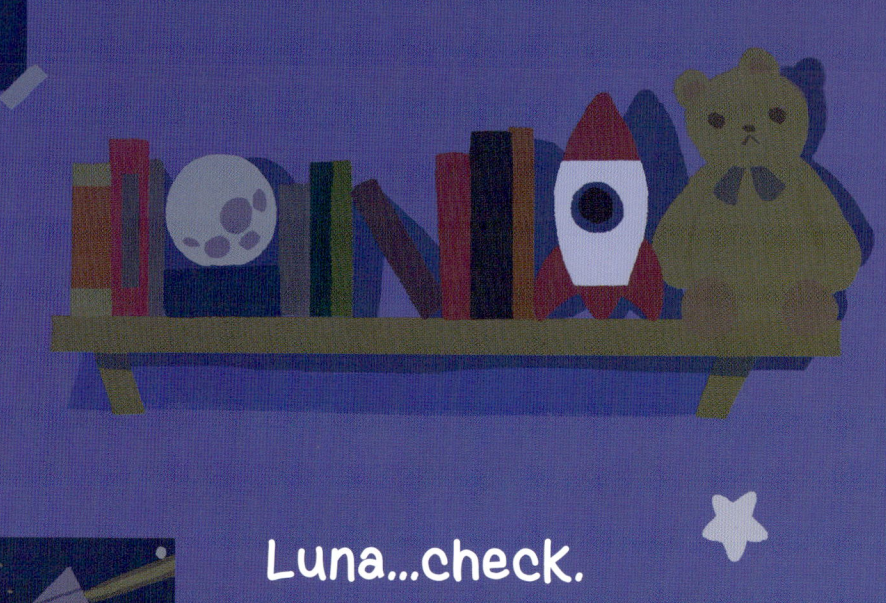

"I'm so sorry sweetie, this is only for the older students."

"You have to be more careful Jurni. Anything could have happened."

"She's always with you, Jurni."

ABOUT THE AUTHOR

NIKOS COX is a designer and photographer currently residing in Northern Virginia. Hailing from Hampton Roads, he has photographed countless future world leaders as a school yearbook photographer, traveled to three continents and ten countries, and helped produce short films and theater productions while studying at Virginia Tech. When he isn't writing, you can find him spending time with family and friends.